It's a CONSPIRACY!

Create your own conspiracy theory for social media

By "Ken Williams"

and "Allison Reeb"

DEDICATION

This book is dedicated to you. The normal, happy, rational, sane, reasonable human being, who can find a bit of humor in the chaos of today's world.

CONTENTS

ACKNOWLEDGMENTS

We'd like to thank Facebook and all the social medias who have created a platform to allow the outer fringe a platform to share their special kind of crazy. Also, thanks to those of you who share the outrageous stuff you share. Without you, this book would not have been necessary.

CHAPTER ONE

EVERYONE LOVES A GOOD
CONSPIRACY

Allegations of conspiracies have been around for hundreds of years. As an example, the Freemasons—since the 1700s—have been shrouded by accusations of conspiracies. Even the term, "Conspiracy Theory" has a conspiratorial tone to it. I'll prove it. Turn to the person sitting next to you and whisper, "It's a Conspiracy Theory." I guarantee that you will get a reaction that will **prove** that the phrase is the result of a conspiracy theory.

The JFK assassination, (heck, even the Lincoln assassination!) the moon landing, Area 51, 5G towers, and dozens of other subjects are the topics of modern conspiracy theories. There are two reasons for this phenomenon:

1) There are plenty of unanswered questions. Incomplete information on news events or new technologies make people uncomfortable. We have been trained by Google to believe that every answer is just a few keystrokes away. The 2020 COVID-19 pandemic, for example is a rich swampland of unanswered questions, making the subject ripe for new theories.

2) People are stupid/gullible/bored

Now, don't get me wrong. I mean that with all the love in my heart and all the kindness I can muster, but look around. (Not at the people in your house…I would *never* say that *they* are stupid. Or gullible. Probably bored, though. I'm talking about everyone else.)

We crave closure. We need to know what happens. That's why there will never be a best-selling book where the ending doesn't wrap up all the loose ends into a tight little package. That's why every Hallmark movie ends with the guy and the girl getting together. Anything else would drive us batty.

When "New" isn't immediately accompanied with "complete, perfect, uncontestable, documented and proven" information, we tend to get edgy. We might not even realize that's the feeling we're having. (Some might call this "anxiety.) We rush to click on our favorite web search engine to get the answers we *deserve to have.* Unfortunately, reliable answers can be hard to come by.

Let me explain.

Let's call "Complete, perfect, uncontestable, documented and proven information," "THE TRUTH." It is true. It is universal. Undeniable.

However, "THE TRUTH." is hard to find on Google because it largely does not exist. And certainly not on Facebook.

What *does* exist on Facebook, however, is "my truth." Do not confuse "THE TRUTH" with "my truth." "My truth is what I believe, based on all the information that I have access to.

I see where you might be confused. "My truth" is frequently disguised as "THE TRUTH" because one time I read an article online, and it was pretty convincing. "My truth," however has alternative facts and opposing opinions. It is not universal and it is **not** undisputable.

Make sense? To avoid confusion, we will refer to "THE TRUTH" as actual TRUTH. Perfect. Indisputable. Universal. Constant. Unchangeable. Uncontestable. True.

"My truth" will be what we believe to be true. Unfortunately, it is imperfect. Disputable. Personal. Flexible, Changeable. Contestable, and not necessarily TRUE. Even though it looks and feels—to us--exactly like THE TRUTH.

Because we have a strong and innate need to plug all of the plot holes that life presents to us, our brains tend to find information to fill in the gaps. Or, our brains may invent information that ties the story together in spite of the holes. It feels much better to us when the holes are plugged (or at least explained), and "my truth" feels lust like THE TRUTH, which means that my truth feels pretty right. And we like being right.

I happen to know this for a fact, because I'm right almost all of the time, and it feels *great!*

So, if you are going to exploit this TRUTH stuff to create your own conspiracy theories, you are well on your way.

Welcome to the armpit of the Internet!

CHAPTER TWO

THE GEARS IN YOUR BRAIN

I'm not a doctor, and I'm not psychic, though I can pretty much guess what you are thinking a lot of the time. I know this because I am a pretty normal person, and you probably are too. For the sake of this chapter, let's just assume that we are reasonable, rational human beings who want to make a difference in this world.

Here's a secret: There are a lot of wackadoodles out there. You probably know a few. I certainly do. They are like squirrels.

Think of the last time you were looking outside the window and saw a squirrel or two trying to hijack seeds for your front yard bird feeder. The squirrel (let's call it Derek) scampers over, looks around cautiously, jumps onto the feeder, fills his pockets with seeds, and looks around guiltily. If Derek sees movement, he will scurry away.

What Derek doesn't know, because his brain is the size of a cashew that has been made into vegan "cheese," is that if he got a couple hundred friends, they could take down your cheap bird feeder, lock you in your house, and abscond with quite the haul. Lucky for you, Derek is easily distracted, and he thinks everyone and everything is out to get him.

Let's use this knowledge to our advantage.

Those wackadoodles I was talking about…they are harmless. They're skittish. They think everyone is out to get them. And if they organized, they could steal your bird feeder and lock you in our house.

We cannot let that happen! The best defense is a good offense, so we are going to create distractions that will keep them busy.

How?

I will tell you. Right now. In this next sentence. Or paragraph.

We will use our knowledge of our need for closure to open up new plot holes, and then fill them in with our own brand of magic.

That's right! Remember how we discussed that you need closure? Guess what! *Everyone else needs closure, too!* That includes the Dereks and other squirrels in the world. They need it as much as you do.

Here's another secret. They may need it more than you and I do. You see, *we* are normal, reasonable, rational human beings. We know that there are unanswered questions. (There are even some unanswerable questions out there.) We may not like it, but we accept that life may get messy, and we may not instantly know everything about everything. We are patient, don't-jump-to-conclusion-able people who can accept an uncomfortable lack of plot occasionally.

But not the Dereks. They need to know.

So, let's tell them. Let's fill in the gaps for them. If we can keep them scurrying from theory to theory, scattering when Mom comes to the window, going ever deeper and deeper into the rabbit hole of crazy, we can keep them from stealing the bird feeders of society.

CHAPTER THREE

A COMMON ENEMY

The first element in creating a good, new conspiracy theory is to find an entity that can be a common enemy.

When you were growing up, Mom and Dad may have been common enemies with you and your siblings. Even though your brother may not have been your favorite person in the world because he got really gassy after eating minestrone soup, you could overlook that sometimes (except on nights when Mom made minestrone for dinner). Maybe he would distract Mom by telling her he wanted to talk about his feelings, while you took the rest of the Tilamook Mudslide ice cream to your room with two spoons so that the two of you could polish off the container. (not based on real events, Mom)

A common enemy unites people. Politically opposed people will overlook differences when there is an enemy that the two sides can agree to hate.

The first step in creating your own conspiracy is to find a common enemy. This is not hard. Look around. They are everywhere.

Political common enemies have been used for decades. In

democratic republics like America, we have often pointed to communist regimes as an enemy. Pro-gun people could be an enemy. Or anti-gun people. Democrats or Republicans. Trump or Biden.

Political targets are easy, but you don't have to stop there. What about science? You have heard of the Scientific Method, which is to develop a hypothesis, experiment and test the hypothesis, and modify the hypothesis as needed. There, of course, is a little bit more to it than that, but I'm not a scientist so it's not really that important. The point is, you can take anything in the middle of Scientific Method testing and you may find a common enemy.

New technologies can be a common enemy. Remember how people get nervous with unanswered questions? New technology brings out plenty of questions, starting with "Is it safe?" and "Will it affect my Internet speed?"

Medicine (not the pills, but the general field of medicine) offers a plethora of common enemies. Cancer. Autism. Overactive bladder.

Money is another differentiator that could be a marker for a common enemy. People who have more than you do—or people who have less than you do—could be the bane of your existence. Not really, because that's crazy talk, but you could make them a common enemy.

And what about Bill? Have you ever known a Bill to be uniter instead of a divider? Bill Gates? Polarizing. Bill Nye? Kind of a scientist, and you know where *that* can lead. Bill Cosby? Yeah. Bill O'Reilly? Bill Maher? Bill Clinton? Exactly my point. There is not a good Bill out there, including your cell phone Bill. (If your name is bill or you know a not evil Bill, I'm not talking about them, of course. Just every other Bill.)

And I shouldn't be doing all this work for you. You should be making up your own conspiracies. I'm just here to get you moving in the right direction.

My point is that you need to start with finding someone or something that a group of people can get behind hating. Or if not hating, not liking. Once you can convince people to not like someone or something, it's a short trip to get them to not trust them.

And the lack of trust is the first step. We are well on our way.

CHAPTER FOUR

WHAT'S YOUR MOTIVATION?

Most people are doing the best they can with the information they have. Maybe you believe me, even though there is plenty of evidence that can be perceived as contrary.

Even the gullible-Americans we all know are trying their hardest. They just don't set the bar very high. Let's go back to how the brain works for a minute.

Stress (or fear) heightens our need for closure and for answers. Because we literally aren't in our right mind, we tend to be more easily influenced during times of stress or fear. Imagine jumping out of an airplane. Probably a highly stressful—or even fearful—moment. I bet it wouldn't' take much for me to convince you that you should OPEN YOUR PARACHUTE! See how this can affect even you and me?

I did a quick Internet search about the ten most common fears in adults, and I found an interesting article from some Australian website. They had a tidy list, and the tenth most common fear in Australia is…trypanophobia, or the fear of needles.

Naturally, because I'm in America, this list is upside down, making the fear of needles *the number one fear of Americans!* Irregardless of my logic, this explains why there are so many needle-related conspiracy theories out there. For example, vaccines.

And the theory that we'll all be marked with secret tattoos after we are appropriately vaccinated. Boom! Double conspiracy!

There are two things at play here. First, the motivation behind the conspiracy. The theories play on our fears. Fear of needles. Of dying. Of being controlled. Of losing freedom. Of there not being any sugar in the pantry when you're ready to start making a chocolate cake.

Second is the motive of the common enemy.

Remember how I said that I believe people are doing the best they can? Well, to make a really convincing conspiracy theory, you have to shift that kind of normal-people thinking into overdrive and assume that *people are out to get you.*

Never mind that you and I—and most normal people— are living such boring lives that *no one in his right mind would have anything to gain by being out to get you*—what would they get anyway?

On the other hand, if **everything** that every one of our common enemies ever did had some ulterior motive, THEN we would be on to something. Once you get into this mindset, it's a short trip to convince people that EVERYONE is up to something nefarious. (That means "bad.")

And since we all want the plot holes of life to be filled in, it's really not that hard to come up with some "nefarious"

(I love that word!) intent for *every single thing*.

Let's try a couple of examples. Remember how Mom made minestrone soup for dinner? Well, of course, she did that because you didn't get great grades last semester, and gassing you out was her way of punishing you.

See? Easy.

Or Mom and Dad didn't proactively give you the rest of the ice cream and you had to sneak it out of the freezer. They told you it was because it was 11:00 PM and past your bedtime, but the only true and logical explanation is that they wanted you to be in bed, asleep, instead.

Nefarious!

It is easy to play on peoples' fears when you help them realize that everyone else is secretly evil. Everyone else except for you, that is. You are the only person who will tell them the truth. You are the only one who can be trusted.

CHAPTER FIVE

JUST THE FACTS

Every three months, a Soyuz vehicle—a rocket—leaves Earth's surface and meets up with the International Space Station to transfer cargo, which may or may not include a Cravings Pack from Taco Bell. The docking procedures involve precise maneuvers, and the final dock has to be accurate within three inches.

Without the limits of gravity, the seven-ton Soyuz is easily steered by small puffs of gas (maybe *that's* what the Taco Bell is for!). My explanation may be a bit simplistic, but the point is it doesn't take a lot to nudge 14,000 pounds to get it moving in the right direction.

By the same token, that gentle nudge, if it were applied at the *wrong* moment, could easily push the Soyuz out of the required orbit, and the poor saps on the International Space Station would never get their Taco Bell.

Our conspiracies shouldn't be huge, ground-breaking revelations. The more outrageous they are, the harder they will be to sell to the masses. No, we just need to gently nudge our soon-to-be followers slightly out of alignment with rational thinking. Let me share a few techniques.

First, people love facts, so we will stick to the facts. People also love pictures, so make sure to attach a picture to your conspiracy claim. The secret, however, is to use a picture that *looks* like it matches the story, but secretly, it nudges thoughts out of alignment.

I can see that you are confused. Let me share an example. Supposed you've chosen GMO (genetically modified organisms) as your common enemy, and you will play on peoples' fears of maintaining good health with the evil GMOs taking over the world. Simply write your assertions and include a stock image of one of those two-headed cows, or maybe a sharktopus image with your story.

Now, technically, you don't actually *say* that GMOs will give cows another head or make octopi turn evil, but the picture will make it easier for gullible-Americans to come to that conclusion on their own. In some cases, they may take up the cause and you won't have to do anything else for that theory to spread. This is the ideal situation because you end up being pretty disconnected from the spread of disinformation.

Secondly, people don't read things too closely, so pull a few words out of an article or journal and let your audience's collective mind interpret things willy-nilly. That is the mark of responsible journalism. We don't tell people what to think. We just tell them what to think about, and let them draw their own conclusions. We're just going to nudge them into thinking what we want them to think.

In practice, this works great with a stock image, but that's not really necessary. Suppose you want to create a panic about people being implanted with microchips to track their whereabouts. Take a legitimate story from a reputable something.gov website that mentions microchips and tracking for vaccines. Never mind that the microchips are designed to be used *on* the vaccines to track the location of the vials, or that the purpose is to track where/when the vaccines were used. By selectively omitting or de-emphasizing relevant facts, you can easily nudge the gullibles.

Finally, don't give this too much thought. Fact-checking is a never-gained art among many of our most gullible. So, yes—give facts when you make claims, but you can usually get away with making them up. Claim to know an eye-witness or someone with personal knowledge of something. Here is where your confidence will overcome almost any roadblock.

The bottom line is that you don't have to *shift* thinking…you just have to *nudge* it a little. Do it early and often enough, and it won't be long before your followers are wildly off course

CHAPTER SIX

CHECK YOUR SOURCES

I went to a magic show with David Copperfield many years ago. Not *with* him, as a magic-show-buddy, but with *him,* as in he was the main act. He has famously vanished a jet, and elephant, and the Statue of Liberty. The secret to these magic tricks is *get people to look at what you want them to see so they don't see the "magic" happen.*

It sometimes takes thousands of pounds of smoke and mirrors, but usually, it's just simple misdirection. He'll get you to look at his right hand while his left hand hides the elephant. You know, stuff like that. Magicians are masters at misdirection. After reading this chapter, you will be, too.

The less gullible Gullible-Americans tend to be suspicious of new claims, so you will need to make it look like you've already done the research. You probably already have, and you certainly don't want the Gullible among us to spend their valuable time reading or learning stuff. Make sure they know that you have done the reading, researching, and thinking for them. Some of these tips will pair up nicely with the nudges we spoke of last chapter.

You may be nervous about linking to a legitimate news story, but remember Copperfield. Watch a couple of magic tricks. Once you know what to look for you can do almost everything out in the open with full confidence that no one will actually follow those links to the news stories. And if they do, they won't actually read the story. And if they do, since you have already nudged them into crazy-thinking with a well-placed and slightly incorrect stock photo, there is almost zero risk of them seeing through your farce.

It will be hilarious!

But just in case, try these bonus tips: First, make sure that any link you share is not clickable. This is super easy if you have something printed on actual paper, like a flyer or a book, but since no one uses those any more, you could be up against a challenge. But you can use that to your advantage. Tell your minions that you went "old school" because The Internet changes things that you post. Trust me. Someone will believe that.

Or, you can just reference the source without providing a specific link. "I read this on whatever.gov." No one will check that. Even if they do, they'll never find the source because you just made it up!

You seem doubtful, but I happen to know that this is true. You can prove it to yourself. Scroll Facebook posts and scan for the phrase, "Snopes says..." or "The CDC says..."

Then search that website for the evidence that the poster promises you will find. I did this twice just today, and both times, the supposed proof from the source website contradicted what the post said.

See? People aren't fact checking their own posts. What makes you think that they will fact check yours?

This is powerful stuff. Get a couple nudges ready and then tell your audience that you've already done the research. Drop a few high-trust sources, like universities, governments, scientists, etc. Match a well-chosen stock picture, and you can tell people almost anything!

Finally, if you're still nervous, just summarize the key facts that support your conspiracy claim. Then the misdirection: Leave out *any contradictory facts*. Your claim gains credibility, you've done the thinking for your cult-like following (and face it…that's what they want anyways), and you have successfully nudged them in the direction you want.

Everyone is a winner. Well, almost everyone.

CHAPTER SEVEN

SPECIFIC AMBIGUITY

My first day as a new manager at my current job was nerve-racking. I imagined that my new group would have high expectations of me and my knowledge. My level of stress intensified as I imagined them coming up to me and asking questions with impossible answers. I would look bad and lose credibility. I took a deep breath and went to my first team meeting.

After introducing myself and stumbling through the content that I had prepared, I asked if anyone needed anything from me. First question: "How much vacation time do I have left?"

I had no idea. I told the team member that I would have to get back to him. Over the next several early days of my new job, I realized that people didn't expect me to have all the answers right now. I could get back to them, and *they were ok with that!*

When you are planning to unleash a new conspiracy theory on the Internet, you may start to feel shortness of breath and feverish. Chances are that's just the coronavirus, but in case it's actual anxiety, rest assured, if someone challenges you on your claims, you have two real and very simple strategies that, I promise, will deflect all the pressure.

Option 1) It is totally OK to say that you are still researching something. Just don't admit that you don't know something, and absolutely don't admit that you were wrong. That's cray-cray.

Over-estimate your knowledge. If you think you read something somewhere, make the bold claim that you *did* read it. How are they going to know? But don't reveal your source. There's some small percentage of thinking people who will want to fact check your claims. Don't give them any ammunition.

"I read this on the government's own website."

See? Nothing too specific. Sounds legit, but impossible to verify.

"It has been thoroughly debunked."

Again. It's an assuring claim, but there's no way that people can counter your assertion.

Option 2) Invoke "Them."

Who are "they?" I have no idea, but "they" are important. "They" are omnipotent and omniscient. "They" don't exist, but "they" don't know that! ("They" are your gullibles who will be falling for your stories, hook, line, and sinker.)

"They" are the source of everything good…or everything bad. And "They" are super credible.

Any claim, any theory, any conspiracy can benefit from "them."

"Three things *they* don't want you to know about the moon

landing." Sounds ominous, and that's almost guaranteed to get some traction.

"They're taking away our rights!" "That's exactly what they want you to believe." "They are censoring my free speech!"

People will assume who "They" are, and almost always it's some common enemy (remember chapter three?) or a real or imagined source (chapter 6).

Seriously. This book isn't that long. If you've already forgotten the brilliant ideas we shared, maybe this isn't right for you.

I'm sorry. I got carried away. I'm a bit hangry, and they said that I would behave better once I eat a bowl of Tillamook Rocky Road ice cream.

Did you believe that? It's a total lie! I don't even like Rocky Road, but when I wrote that "they" said it, you automatically believed it.

This is powerful stuff. Just don't let it get into the wrong hands. If it does, I can't be held responsible.

CHAPTER EIGHT

THE CIRCULAR LOGIC MACHINE GUN

One of the most beautiful words in the English language is "Irregardless." Mostly because my mother-in-law hates it, but irregardless, I love to use it whenever I can. It always makes me smile when I hear it.

Imagine asking someone less smarter than you to define "irregardless." Because of their stunted intellectual capacity, they will probably say that "irregardless" means "not regardless." The prefix "ir" means not. Just like those "Irregular" jeans means they're "not regular," and they probably have the button fly installed horizontally.

But defining a word by using the word isn't all that helpful if you don't' know what the word means in the first place. And that's where the power lies. It's an example of circular logic.

If you are a user of spreadsheets, you can imagine "circular logic" as being a cell with a formula that references itself. For example, cell A1=A1+A2.

Excel will stress out, because whatever is in A2, when you add it to A1 to put the result in A1, you now change A!, and that changes the result. Which again changes A1, and that changes the result. For infinity.

So, what does this mean for you? If someone is not a master spreadsheeter, they may not even notice the circular reasoning error unless a smart person like you or me points it out. It will fly under the radar, as they say. So, you should use circular logic in your use of conspiracy theories. People will be none the wiser.

One of the hardest arguments to win is when someone points out positive proof that your conspiracy is false. Actual data that negates your entire argument.

Fear not. Circular Logic Man (or woman) to the rescue. All you have to do is say about that source that "they are part of the conspiracy."

See? Brilliant! If you can claim that all legitimate sources of information are a part of the massive coverup, you can say *anything* and there is no defense.

"Snopes says the exact opposite of what you claim." My answer to that? "Well, I would believe that *if* Snopes weren't being paid off by (insert common enemy)."

If that doesn't fully kill the challenge, then you can use what I call the Machine Gun Approach. I have seen this work successfully dozens of times. (Well, twice. But that's a pretty good track record.)

When you shoot a machine gun, the rounds hit the target, rapid-fire. The victim doesn't have time to respond to any given impact, and you eventually overwhelm the poor sap, and he gives up. I am not speaking from experience, in case you were concerned. I just saw this in a movie once.

You want to create a rapid-fire series of doubts, and all you need to do is machine gun as many arguments as possible, as quickly as possible. No need to listen to their voice of reason. Overwhelm them with your constant punches to the gut of "facts" and "concerns." It will become overwhelming, and the fact that you have dozens of possible evidences may be enough to convince them to listen to you.

And as a final statement, feel free to borrow a line that I'm paraphrasing form that guy who made that movie. "Well, maybe that's not *exactly* how it is, but *something's* not right."

Remember? Just a little nudge. You just want to create a shadowy doubt. That's all there is to it.

If you can get someone to find an enemy amongst the people they thought they could trust, they will start to distrust everyone. And creating a society of people who can't, don't, or won't engage in trust with each other makes it that much easier for the *real* conspiracies to be propagated.

Thank you, and welcome to the club.

.

ABOUT THE AUTHORS

Ken has been happily married to the same woman since 1990, and he is the father of five children. He is a published author, an amazing teacher, and one of the nicest people you'll ever meet. He is an expert at making chocolate cake, and he has the recipe memorized. Ken is the author of the Amazon best-selling business books <u>21 Days to Success through Networking</u> and <u>21 Days to Success with LinkedIn</u> as well as the less-than-helpful grammar book, <u>Irregardless,</u> and the real-life Christmas story, <u>The Christmas Clock.</u> You should probably buy them all.

Allison is either his favorite or second favorite daughter, depending on who is asking. She graduated with a degree in biology, so she knows lots of sciency stuff. She is married to the future Dr. Reeb, who is attending a special quarantine version of dental school. She co-wrote Irregardless, and she is the inspiration behind "It's a Conspiracy"